THOSE
AMAZING
BATS

Cheryl M. Halton

Dillon Press
New York

Acknowledgments

The author wishes to thank Dr. Merlin Tuttle, Pat Morton, and Mari Murphy, of Bat Conservation International, for all of the information and help they so freely shared and for the extraordinary work they do to protect bats worldwide.

All photographs are reproduced through the courtesy of Merlin D. Tuttle, Bat Conservation International, except for the photos of Pe'a' the flying fox, by William E. Rainey, and of Dr. Charles Campbell's bat tower, from Express News Corp.

Library of Congress Cataloging-in-Publication Data

Halton, Cheryl M. (Cheryl Mays)
  Those amazing bats : Cheryl M. Halton.
     p.   cm.
  Includes bibliographical references and index.
  Summary: Describes the varieties, behavior, and benefits of bats and explains why people fear them.
  ISBN 0-87518-458-8 (lib. bdg.)
  1. Bats—Juvenile literature. [1. Bats.] I. Title.
  QL737.C5H34   1991
  599.4—dc20   90-3959
                                                          CIP
                                                          AC

Macmillan Publishing Company, 866 Third Avenue
New York, NY 10022

Printed in the United States of America
  2 3 4 5 6 7 8 9 10

Contents

Dr. Merlin Tuttle and a guard enter a bat cave in Thailand.

1 Gentle Creatures of the Night

Dr. Merlin Tuttle sat alone and very still in the darkness, deep in the jungle on a moonless night. Waiting, he listened intently for any sound.

Earlier, officials had forbidden him to enter the Khao Yai National Park in Thailand at night without armed guards. Antigovernment guerrillas patrolled the area. Dangerous tigers roamed freely. One had recently crashed through a window at park headquarters and killed a ranger.

The night before, guards did accompany the now lone scientist. Still, they refused to go with him into a dense stand of banana trees. They feared that 15-foot (4.6-meter) king cobras as big around as a man's leg would be lurking there.

When Dr. Tuttle, one of the world's leading bat

6

experts, heard a twig snap, his nerves tingled, and sweat beaded on his forehead. He reviewed his escape plans. Suddenly, leaves rustled close by. With a rush the jungle parted as his assistant and one guard appeared. Seeing them, Tuttle sighed with relief. The assistant had left hours before to bring the guards. Only one, though, had agreed to return. The others thought it was too dangerous!

Tuttle had gone into the jungle in daylight to set up three 40-foot (12.2-meter) **mist nets**. These nets are made of fine mesh that is hardly visible. Now Tuttle watched them, hoping to capture not cobras, tigers, or gun-toting men, but bats. He needed bats in order to photograph and study them.

Dr. Tuttle, his assistant, and the armed guard continued to wait for an hour in the darkness. The nets, strung across elephant trails, finally did the job. High-pitched squeaks and the sound of flapping wings alerted Tuttle that a bat was in the net. He turned on his headlamp and gently lifted the small creature with brown fur and pointy ears out of the net. Bright little eyes stared at Tuttle as the bat

As Thai guards watch, Dr. Merlin Tuttle lifts a bat out of a mist net.

struggled to get away. The frightened animal was so small that it easily fit in the scientist's hand. He could feel the rapid beat of its heart as he untangled the feet and wings caught in the net.

Tuttle knew the bat posed no threat to him or anyone else. He gently stroked the animal as he looked at it more carefully. Then he lifted it clear of the net and let it fly away. The bat was not the

8

species, or kind, for which Tuttle was looking.

The men waited and listened a while longer. Finally, they folded up the nets, gathered their photographic equipment, and hiked out of the jungle. They would have to try again another night.

Fear of Bats

Dr. Tuttle and other scientists are concerned about threats to bats and are trying to learn new ways to protect them. People in many countries fear and hate bats because they believe them harmful. In some areas people are killing bats at alarming rates.

The loathing of bats began in ancient times when people feared the night. To them, darkness meant witches, demons, and evil spirits. Because bats are **nocturnal**, or active at night, people believed they took part in evil activities that happened when most people slept.

Bats have often been pictured as evil, beast-like creatures in the myths and folktales of Japan, the Philippines, Africa, Europe, the Middle East, and the Americas. Indians of Guyana, a South American country, repeat a folktale about an enormous bat that lived in the mountains. At night the bat swooped down on the village and with huge claws grabbed anyone it found outside. The bat carried the unlucky person to its nest on Bat Mountain, where the victim was eaten.

The ancient Mayans of Central America believed the bat was actually a god. This bat god had tremendous power and controlled both the Underworld and the Kingdom of Darkness and Death.

Today, many people still are afraid of bats. They may not believe in witches, demons, or bat gods, but they believe bats will bite or hurt them. In fact, bats are shy and avoid people. Even sick bats rarely attack unless they are threatened.

However, if you find a bat on the ground or in the open, do not pick it up or handle it. It is likely that the bat is sick or injured. A bat or any other animal behaving strangely could have rabies, a deadly disease. But bats do not get rabies more often than other wild animals.

"Only ten people in the United States and

10

Canada have contracted rabies from bats in more than thirty years," said Dr. Tuttle. "Many more people are killed yearly by dog attacks, bee stings, power mowers, or lightning than have been killed by rabid bats over the past thirty years."

Respect for Bats

While people in many cultures fear bats, others believe bats bring good luck and happiness. The Chinese word for bat is *fu*. Although spelled differently, the Chinese word for happiness is also pronounced *fu* (as spelled in the Roman alphabet). In China, bats are used frequently in the design of fabrics, ceramics, jewelry, art, and toys. In fact, images of bats were used in the design of the emperor's throne.

The most common Chinese bat design is the *wu-fu*. Five bats, wings outstretched and touching, encircle a symbol of the tree of life. The wu-fu design is a symbol for the five blessings of health, wealth, long life, good luck, and happiness.

Centuries ago, in medieval times, many families in England, France, Germany, and Switzerland used

The most common Chinese bat design, the wu-fu *(above, left), and the blazon for the city of Valencia, Spain (above, right) show respect for bats.*

bat designs on their coat-of-arms. Such designs also formed part of the blazon, or symbol, for the cities of Valencia and Barcelona, Spain.

More recently, bats have received some positive attention through *Batman*, the movie. Dr. Paul Robertson, an environmental science professor at Trinity University in San Antonio, says the movie "shows the bat as a symbol of goodness and strength."

The Flying Mammal

Most people believe bats are either birds or flying mice. They are neither. Bats, like cats, dogs, horses, cows, and humans, are **mammals.** Bats are the only mammals that can truly fly. Other animals such as flying squirrels merely glide on flaps of skin after leaping off a high perch. Unlike bats, they do not have wings and cannot lift themselves into the air.

Because they are mammals, bats are born live, not hatched from eggs like birds. Instead of feathers, bats have furry bodies. Also, like some other mammals, bats have an arm, wrist, and hand with a thumb and four fingers. But in bats, the bones of the hand and fingers are very long and form the structure of the wings.

Bats' legs are different from those of other mammals. They hook to the hip so that the knees point backward instead of forward when they bend. This arrangement helps bats when they fly in for a landing, because they do a little flip in the air and come to rest upside down!

Bats around the World

The largest numbers of bats live in the tropics, where there is plenty of food year round. Yet they are found in all land areas of the earth except the Arctic and Antarctic, some extreme desert areas, and a few remote islands. They are common in lowlands as well as in mountainous areas.

Bats vary greatly in size, color, and habits. They

Bats can fly because the bones of the hand and fingers are very long and form the structure of the wings.

range from the tiny bumblebee bats of Thailand, which weigh less than a penny, to the largest flying foxes of the tropics, which have a wingspan of nearly 6 feet (1.8 meters). Most bats, though, measure about 8 to 12 inches (20 to 30.5 centimeters) from wing tip to wing tip, and weigh less than an ounce.

Some bats that live in the open and roost in trees or buildings have brightly colored fur and showy markings. These markings help bats to blend in with the places where they roost. Bats that live in dark, sheltered areas such as caves or attics are usually less colorful.

Most species of bats eat night-flying insects. Others are fruit eaters, and some are **carnivorous**. They eat small frogs, fish, lizards, rodents, birds, and even other bats. Vampire bats feed on the blood of other animals. But these creatures live only in Mexico and in Central and South America. They are not found in the United States.

Bats are gentle animals that help create a healthy environment for people. Not only do they eat tremendous numbers of insects, they carry pollen from one plant to another. In this way, they help new plants to grow. They also spread seeds of many plants valuable to humans. Increasingly, they are important to medical researchers and other scientists as well. These researchers study bats to develop ways to help blind people move from place to place, low temperature surgery techniques, and new **vaccines** (killed or weakened germs that are injected into people to protect them from certain illnesses).

Scientists are eager to tell people about the important role bats play in our environment and in science. They believe that with better understanding, people worldwide will work to protect these often misunderstood and mistreated animals.

2 Bats Large and Small

Bats are ancient animals. They have filled the night skies for the past 60 million years. And yet, some of the earliest fossil forms are remarkably similar to those that live today.

There are more than 950 species of bats worldwide. They make up one-fourth of all mammals on earth, and almost half the mammals in the tropics.

Because they are such unusual animals, scientists have placed bats in a group of their own. They make up the order **Chiroptera**, which means hand-wing. The wing of a bat is much like the hand of a human, but it is much larger in proportion to the bat's small body. Unlike birds, bats can move the bones of their wings individually, and can change the shape of their wings rapidly. As a result, they can dive, hover, turn sharply, and perform acrobatic feats birds could never match.

Bats use their wings for more than flying. They also help bats to capture flying insects, to keep warm while roosting in cool temperatures, and to get rid of excess heat in warm weather. Folded, the wings look much like crepe paper with many tiny wrinkles, pleats, and tucks. These pleats and tucks help the wings to gather into neat folds when the bats are resting.

Bats' thumbs vary from one species to another. In some, they are small and hardly used. In others, they are larger and serve as hooks to help bats crawl. Thumbs also help bats to hold food while they eat.

When bats are not flying, they usually hang upside down. Scientists believe that roosting head down allows bats to make use of space that is unavailable to birds or other creatures. They can cling to rock crevices, cave ceilings, and similar places that other animals cannot use. In addition, this is an excellent position from which to fly and

rapidly pick up speed. Bats have strong toes which grip tightly to tree branches, grooves in rocks, or other rough surfaces. Their hold can be so strong that even in death they may remain attached to their roost.

The Chiroptera are divided into two groups or suborders: **Megachiroptera** (megabats), which means large hand-wing, and **Microchiroptera** (microbats), which means small hand-wing. These two kinds of bats are as distantly related to each other as a Siberian tiger is to a California sea otter. New research even suggests that the megabats may be our distant relatives. Humans are **primates** (as are apes and monkeys). Some scientists believe megabats are also primates because their brain pathways are similar to those all primates have.

Megachiroptera (Megabats)

Megabats are commonly called flying foxes because their faces look so much like the face of a fox or dog. They have large eyes and a doglike mouth or muzzle. Some megabats, which are

Like other bats, these Gambian epauleted bats roost hanging upside down.

usually larger than microbats, weigh as much as two pounds (nearly one kilogram). These are frequently called fruit bats because they eat only fruit, or the **nectar** and **pollen** from flowers. Nectar is a sweet, sometimes sticky liquid produced by flowers. Pollen is most often a yellowish powder that contains the male reproductive cells of a plant.

Megabats differ from all other bats in some important ways. Their wing design is simple compared to other bats, and their flight styles are less acrobatic. Still, they are strong fliers, capable of traveling long distances for both food and shelter. Sometimes they fly as far as 20 miles (32 kilometers) to a favorite eating ground.

Megabats have much larger eyes than other bats. They use their excellent eyesight and keen sense of smell to navigate, or find their way, in the dark, and to find food.

Megabats are very social animals. They like to roost in large groups or colonies, sometimes called camps. Though these bats usually gather in trees, some find suitable caves. Thousands are known to

A straw-colored flying fox, or megabat.

gather in one area, where they make such loud chat-
tering noises that they can be heard a mile away.
Sometimes so many hang from the limbs of trees
that the weight causes the branches nearly to touch
the ground. When the food supply in the surrounding

area has been used up, they often move to another camp. However, some colonies have been known to remain as long as fifty years in one roost.

The largest fruit bats are found in Southeast Asia, the Indonesian island of Java, and the Philippines. These are the ones with the 6-foot (1.8-meter) wingspans. They are also the most doglike in appearance.

Another large species, which has a wingspread of more than 3 feet (.9-meter), is found in Africa. Called the "hammer-head" or "horse-faced" bat, these bats have large, wide muzzles with bumpy lips. They are especially fond of fruit juice, but are best known for the loud noises they make as they fly through the jungles late at night.

Though most megabats are large, a few species are small. Some are small enough to fit in the palm of an adult's hand.

Many of the smaller megabats are nectar and pollen eaters. When they feed, they stick their long snouts down in flowers. Some even have long, brush-like tongues well adapted to lapping up nectar.

Microchiroptera (Microbats)

Most microbats are much smaller than megabats. They are found worldwide and include many families of bats with a wide range of characteristics. Most of them eat insects. The others feed on fruit, small animals, other bats, or blood.

While the megabats are known for their appealing, doglike faces, microbats are often said to look scary or freakish. They have big ears, small eyes, and oddly shaped noses. Many species of microbats have large flaps or folds of skin on their faces known as **nose leaves**. Others have large bumps or pieces of skin that project outward at odd angles. Some even have slits or deep hollows on their foreheads. According to scientists, these facial features help bats to navigate and find food. But to people who have not seen them before, they do indeed look strange.

All bats in both North and South America are microbats. In the United States and Canada, there are forty-two species of microbats. These vary in size, color, habits, and appearance.

Microbats such as this red bat have big ears, small eyes, and oddly shaped noses.

Many are seldom seen by people. Some live in isolated areas far away from towns and cities. Others have decreased in number so that encounters with people are rare. Some species of microbats that are more frequently seen are described below.

Big Brown Bats *(Eptesicus fuscus)*

These bats are found in nearly all of the United States, parts of Canada, and South America. They have a deep brown color and a wing-span of about 12 inches (30.5 centimeters).

Big brown bats often live in colonies in attics, wall spaces, hollow trees, caves, or mines. They eat a variety of insects but are especially fond of

This big brown bat has caught a tasty moth.

beetles. These hardy bats can withstand subfreez-
ing temperatures and often remain in attics throughout the winter.

Mexican Free-Tailed Bats *(Tadarida brasiliensis)*

There are six species of free-tailed bats in the
United States, but only the Mexican free-tailed bat
is commonly seen. These bats live in the southern
half of the United States and in Mexico and Central
America. Most are found only in about a dozen
caves. They form the largest colonies of any warm-
blooded animal.

The largest of all bat colonies—more than 20
million bats—lives in Bracken Cave near San Antonio, Texas. Another Texas colony, of at least
750,000 bats, is found under the Congress Avenue
Bridge in downtown Austin. It is the largest urban
bat colony in the world. People often gather at dusk
at the roosting sites of Mexican free-tailed bats.
They watch as huge columns of flying bats emerge
from their roosts and fill the darkening sky like columns of smoke climbing toward the horizon.

Mexican free-tailed bats leave their roosting colony at Frio Cave.

It takes nearly four hours for all the bats to leave Bracken Cave. Each night from March to October, they eat more than 250,000 pounds (112,500 kilograms) of insects. Their evening meal is equal to the weight of about twenty-five fully grown elephants.

These bats fly south for the winter. Some travel 1,000 to 1,500 miles (1,600 to 2,400 kilometers) to their winter home.

The hoary bat gets its name from the white tips on its deep brown fur.

Hoary Bats *(Lasiurus cinereus)*

The hoary bat is found in all fifty U.S. states, South America, most of Canada, Iceland, and some Caribbean islands. The bat gets its name from the white tips on its deep brown fur. These white tips give the bat a frosty or hoary look.

With a wingspan of nearly 16 inches (40.5 centimeters), hoary bats are among the largest bats found in North America. They are also among the most attractive, with white markings on wrists, black fur on the rims of their ears, and yellow fur circling their throat.

These bats do not form colonies. They do group together during mating season and when they **migrate**, or move, to warmer climates. Hoary bats usually roost in tree foliage, and rarely in buildings or attics.

Red Bats *(Lasiurus borealis)*

Red bats are common to most of Canada, the United States, and South America. They have long, soft fur that ranges from bright orange to yellowish brown. Their long, narrow wings measure about 11 inches (28 centimeters) from tip to tip.

These bats do not form colonies except during mating season and migration. At other times they roost hidden in the leaves of trees. Because they

usually hang from one foot and wrap themselves in their wings, they are often mistaken for a dead leaf. This helps to protect them from the hawks or blue-jays that often hunt them.

Red bats are among the fastest flying bats. Scientists say they can reach speeds of more than 40 miles (65 kilometers) per hour. Most other bats fly between 5 and 8 miles (8 to 13 kilometers) per hour.

Mouse-Eared Bats *(Myotis)*

Of the fifteen species of mouse-eared bats that are found north of Mexico, most are so secretive that they are rarely seen by people. Only the little brown bat *(Myotis lucifugus)*, which often roosts in buildings, is commonly observed.

Little brown bats are so skilled at capturing their food that scientists say some can catch as many as 600 mosquitoes in an hour.

Mouse-eared bats found in North America range from brown or reddish brown to gray. They have a wingspan that is usually less than 7.5 inches (19 centimeters).

The red bat is often mistaken for a dead leaf because it usually wraps itself in its wings while hanging from one foot.

A little brown bat roosts in a cave.

During the winter, mouse-eared bats **hibernate** in caves or abandoned mines. During this time, all of their body functions slow down. They are in a resting state and do not eat. Instead, they live off stores of body fat.

Pallid Bats *(Antrozous pallidus)*

Pallid bats are found in Mexico, in the southwest-

These pallid bats roost in a barn.

ern United States, and in Nevada, Oregon, and Washington. These medium-sized bats are usually light in
color. Most have yellow or cream-colored fur on their
backs, and white fur on their chest and abdomen.

Pallid bats eat insects found on the ground,
such as crickets, beetles, grasshoppers, and even
scorpions. They often live in caves or rock crevices
in small groups ranging from 12 to 100 bats.

Silver-Haired Bats *(Lasionycteris noctivigans)*

Silver-haired bats are found in most parts of the United States and Canada, though they are rare in the southwestern and gulf states. They are known for their black or dark brown fur. On the fur of their backs, they have silvery tips.

During the summer, silver-haired bats live in trees, rock crevices, under tree bark, and even in woodpecker holes. They are also found in carports, sheds, and other open buildings. These slow-flying bats often hunt for insects over ponds and streams in wooded areas.

Other Bat Species

Only a few of the more than 950 species of bats have been mentioned. Little is known about most of them, because their secretive and solitary ways make study difficult. Scientists are working hard to learn more about bats. Some scientists are especially interested in how bats raise their young.

A silver-haired bat roosts on a tree.

3

Raising Young

Bats are a very large group of animals that differ in many ways. For example, there are differences in the way they behave during courtship, mating, and raising of young.

In some species, males and females avoid each other except during mating season. In others, the males guard the best feeding sites and allow only females that mate with them to feed. Females of some species choose mates whose voice or dance appeals to them.

In most cases, bats mate and then go their separate ways. A few tropical species, though, are thought to mate for life. Among other species, the males of large colony-forming groups often live hundreds of miles from the females for most of the year. This reduces the competition for food near areas where the females are raising young. But in some species that live in small groups or pairs, males stay with the females and help to protect and raise young bats.

Young Bats

Many bats of North America mate in the fall or winter. But the sperm from the male may be held in the female's body for months before it **fertilizes** the egg, and a baby bat begins to form within the mother.

Scientists believe that this waiting period occurs because the courtship patterns require a great deal of energy. During the late summer and early fall, bats are storing fat for the winter. They have adequate reserves that enable them to engage in courtship and mating. During the winter, they use up the stored fat when food is not available. By early spring, they often are too weak for anything other than finding food. When conditions improve for the mother, the egg and sperm join. Young microbats

Mexican free-tailed baby bats.

begin to grow inside the mother. In two or three months—usually in May or June—they are born.

In most cases, a mother gives birth to just one pup. Twins are common in some kinds of bats. In a few species, three or four pups are sometimes born to one mother.

Before their babies are born, female bats of some species group together in **nursery colonies**.

These may be special areas within a cave or attic that are already used as roosts by both male and female bats. Or, they may be established at other sites where only the females go to give birth. Either way, the nursery colonies must be in a very warm and humid environment. Males of some species leave at this time to live by themselves in caves, trees, buildings, or rock crevices.

As soon as the baby is born, the mother nurses her young. Mothers of some species then place the newborns in a group called a **creche**. Thousands of furless newborns hang from the walls and ceilings in a mass. As many as 5,000 young bats can crowd into just one square yard on the cave's ceiling. Their constant, high-pitched squeaks can be heard even from outside the roost.

The huge number of animals packed into a small area, along with their droppings, or **guano**, can raise the temperature inside the cave to more than 100°F (38°C). This warm environment is just what newborns need. But if a baby bat loses its grip, it falls into the guano. There it is quickly

A mother among a group of baby Mexican free-tailed bats.

eaten by beetles and other insects that also thrive in the heat and the nutrient-rich pile of droppings.

Until recently, scientists believed that mothers returned to the creche every few hours to nurse any of the thousands of hungry pups. But research has proved that bat mothers locate their own pup among the thousands clustered together. Each baby bat has not only a distinctive odor, but it has a distinctive call or voice as well.

Young bats move about within a small area of the creche while the mothers roost in another area of the cave. Before the mothers go out for their nightly search for insects, they usually nurse their young. Sometimes they return several times during the night. Then, when they return in the morning, they nurse the babies again. The mothers call out as they climb over hundreds of babies in search of their own pups. They listen for and recognize the high-pitched squeaks of their pups.

Some larger species of bats, such as flying foxes, carry their newborns with them while they fly the night skies in search of food. The baby clings to the mother's breast and fur. It rides along each night until it is too heavy to be carried.

Most baby bats nurse for one to three months. During this time they must learn to fly and to hunt for food on their own. They must also learn to avoid **predators**, animals that will eat them if given the chance. Bat predators include owls, snakes, large fish, and even other bats.

42

Young bats and mothers roost in the nursery cave all summer. They eat as much as possible during this time, building up their fat reserves to prepare for winter.

Bats in Winter

As the weather begins to cool in the fall, the males, females, and young of some species of

A bat mother with a nursing baby.

bats fly south to warmer climates. Mexican free-tailed bats, which are common in southwestern parts of the United States, spend the winter in central Mexico. Some bats from as far north as Canada migrate south to Mexico for the winter.

Other bats hibernate during cold weather. These species usually travel less than 300 miles (480 kilometers) from their summer homes to caves or mines that are neither too warm nor too cold during winter. For three or four months, they hang from the cave walls and live off their stored fat. If bats are disturbed by just one cave explorer while they are hibernating, they use up their fat reserves too quickly. These reserves cannot be replaced during winter because their food sources are not available. As a result, the disturbed bats often die.

During hibernation, bats are in a resting state. Their heartbeat slows from about 400 beats to about 25 beats per minute. Their breathing and all other bodily functions slow as well. In fact, their temperature drops as much as 50°F (10°C). By the time they come out of hibernation in the spring, they

44

have lost one-third or more of their body weight.

Bats that live in areas that are warm year round have no need to migrate or hibernate. They have a constant food supply and often give birth twice a year.

For their size, bats are not only the slowest reproducing animals on earth, they are among the most long-lived animals. Some have survived more than thirty years. Whether they hibernate or migrate, bats are extremely loyal to both their summer and winter homes. Year after year, they return to the same sites. How bats find their way over the long distances they travel remains a mystery. Most scientists believe they use landmarks such as mountain ranges, coastlines, or large rivers to guide them on their journey.

For many years people also wondered how bats could navigate in the dark and capture insects so tiny that they could hardly be seen. Not until this century did scientists begin to solve this difficult puzzle.

4

"Seeing" With Sound

For hundreds of years—probably thousands—people have known that bats fly very well at night. Rarely do they run into trees, buildings, cliffs, cave walls, or other obstacles. Even on the darkest night, bats can detect objects as small as a gnat or as fine as a human hair.

Solving a Scientific Puzzle

At first, people thought bats had unusually sharp vision. But in the late 1700s, an Italian scientist, Lazzaro Spallanzani, proved this theory wrong.

Spallanzani was interested in the night vision of many animals. He kept a variety of animals that are active at night in his laboratory. One evening he was watching an owl fly about the room. The owl accidentally flew too close to the candle that was lighting the laboratory and blew out the flame. Immediately, the owl crashed into the wall. It was unable to fly in total darkness. Spallanzani decided to see how bats would fare in similar conditions. To his amazement, they had no trouble at all flying in darkness without bumping into walls and other obstacles. The scientist, puzzled, decided to study the eyes of both bats and owls. But he could find nothing to explain the difference.

Next, Spallanzani decided to blind the bats (an act most people today would consider inhumane). Even blinded, the bats had no trouble flying. In fact, they were able to avoid slender threads Spallanzani had hung at odd angles from the ceiling. Still puzzled, Spallanzani released the bats to see if they would be able to catch food. Several days later he returned to the site where he had first captured the bats. There in the colony were the blinded bats. Once again, he captured them and examined the contents of their stomachs. The bats had eaten just as many insects as the bats with normal vision. Spallanzani realized then that bats did not rely on sight for navigation or feeding.

Other tests he performed showed that bats need hearing to fly and to feed. But he could not understand how hearing alone could guide bats. Spallanzani decided that bats must have an undiscovered "sixth sense" which he was unable to explain.

Other scientists rejected Spallanzani's claims and said bats relied on touch. The "touch theory" held for more than a century. Then, in the early 1900s, scientists decided that bats detected echoes of sounds produced by the flapping of their own wings.

In 1938, Donald Griffin, a Harvard University biology student who studied bats, learned about equipment newly invented by G.W. Pierce, a Harvard physics professor. The device could pick up high-frequency sounds that humans cannot hear. Griffin decided to take several of his bats in a cage to Pierce's office to find out if bats made high-frequency sounds. When the bats were placed next to the machine, Griffin heard high-pitched squeaking noises. When the machine was turned off, he could no longer hear the sounds.

Griffin determined that bats do rely on sound to navigate, communicate, and capture insects. But bats do not produce the sound by flapping their wings. Bats send out high-frequency signals either through their mouths or noses. They produce sounds in rapid bursts—as many as 250 beeps per second. When these sound waves hit an object, they bounce back to the bats as echoes. The bats pick up the echoes with their large, movable ears. From the echoes, bats can determine the size, shape, texture, and distance of objects.

Bats can change the speed and pitch—the highness or lowness—of the sounds they make to provide even more clues about the objects around them. For example, bats can tell if an insect is soft and hairy like a caterpillar, or hard like a beetle. They can even compare the speed of flying insects with their own flight speeds. They then know how long it will take to reach the insects. Bats' ability to find their way or their food by

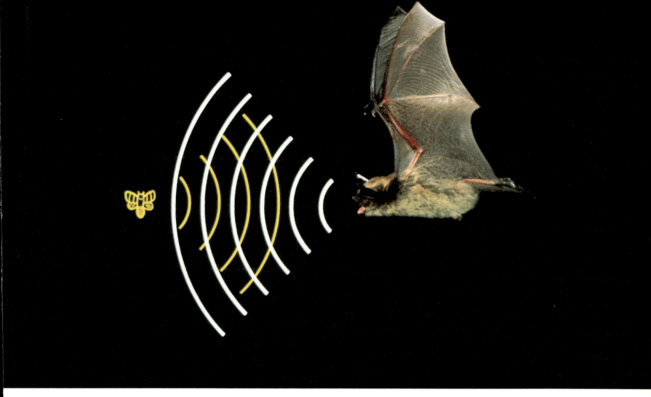

This photograph and diagram of a little brown bat in flight show how the bat uses echolocation to capture insects.

listening to echoes of sounds they make is called **echolocation**.

The Amazing, Echolocating Bat

Bats are not the only animals that echolocate. Other animals with this ability include dolphins, whales, some birds, and little insect-eating animals called shrews.

While all microbats echolocate, only one type of megabat has this ability. Most megabats are fruit eaters and rely instead on their excellent vision and sense of smell to find food. Insect-eating bats, on the other hand, need echolocating ability to find tiny insects in the dark. Echolocation works best when used to find small objects that are nearby—usually within 10 feet (3.1 meters) of the bat. Microbats also use their vision to detect enemies and to fly long distances to migrate or reach a feeding area.

In one way, echolocation makes feeding more difficult for bats. Some insects can hear the high-frequency sounds they make.

Many species of moths, green lacewings, crickets, mantids, and some katydids are warned in advance of the bats' approach by the high-pitched squeaks they are making. Some moths take quick action to avoid bats by darting to the side, just out of reach as the bats fly by. Grasshoppers and other insects often stay near the ground and hide under leaves or grass when possible. But bats have a few tricks, too. Not only can they do flips and sharp

A pallid bat captures a katydid.

turns in the air, but bats use their wings like nets to scoop up **prey** and direct it toward their mouths.

Scientists believe that the special ability to echolocate gives some microbats their unusual appearance. Large nose leaves and other fleshy facial features may help direct the sound bats produce away from themselves. The folds and flaps may help protect their ears from sounds the bats send so that they can better pick up the returning echoes.

Scientists do not know exactly how this system of echolocation in bats works. They do know bats use it to navigate and to communicate with each other. It is a natural **sonar system**, similar to the echo system used by ships to detect underwater objects such as submarines, icebergs, and schools of fish. But the bat's sonar system, according to Dr. Merlin Tuttle, "far surpasses [goes beyond] current scientific understanding." He notes that, "on a watt-per-watt, ounce-by-ounce basis [the bat's sonar system] has been estimated to be billions of times more efficient than any similar system developed by humans."

Scientists such as Dr. William O'Neill of the University of Rochester Center for Brain Research are studying the ways bats make use of the echoes created by the sounds they produce. The researchers have found that different parts of bats' brains interpret different parts of the echo. Some brain nerve cells respond to changes in tone or frequency. Others respond to the time span between sounds.

Scientists are conducting studies to find out if the human brain also has special regions for interpreting the sounds of speech. They still have much more work to do before they know the answer, says Dr. O'Neill. But they have found that humans can use sound to find their way to a far greater degree than had been known earlier.

As a result of this research, a device for the blind has been developed that uses sonar similar to bats' sonar. The device sends out sounds that bounce off objects. Differences in the echoes can be used by blind people to determine the size, distance, and location of objects. This can help them get around without bumping into objects in their path.

Bats are important to many types of scientists in addition to those who study their sonar system. Physicians, biologists, botanists, and others are beginning to focus their research on bats. Some study the effects of bats on the environment.

5 Bats in Science and the Environment

 Bats are essential to the well-being of our planet. Without them, thousands of species of animals and plants could die out. Areas of the earth as different as rain forests and deserts depend on them.

Today, bats are the least studied of all mammals. But they are gaining new interest and attention as scientists around the world recognize their importance.

Bats and Scientific Research

Many colonies of bats inhabit the same roosts year after year. When thousands or millions of bats gather in large colonies, one result is a huge supply of guano on the roost's floor.

Bat guano is rich in saltpeter, a substance used

to make several types of explosives. During the American Civil War, Confederate soldiers used it to make gunpowder. Caves with large supplies of guano were closely guarded to protect this valuable natural resource.

Even today, bat guano is harvested and used by farmers and gardeners as an excellent, nutrient-rich fertilizer. One scientist, Dr. Bernie Steele of Auburn University, has a different use for it. He has been studying the **bacteria**, or tiny plants, that are found in bat guano.

All mammals, including bats, have bacteria in their intestines to help them break down and digest food. This bacteria passes out of the intestines along with waste products. Some types of bacteria that Dr. Steele has found in bat guano appear to be completely new species that scientists have never seen before. Some produce **enzymes**, natural substances that cause or speed up reactions in living things. These enzymes may prove to be useful in cleaning up industrial wastes that pollute lakes and streams.

56

Ammonia is a chemical that forms a large part of industrial and municipal waste. When it is dumped into rivers and lakes, it reduces the amount of oxygen in the water. Lack of oxygen kills fish and other wildlife. But the enzymes produced by the bacteria in bat guano may prove useful in removing the ammonia in the waste before it ever reaches lakes and rivers.

Other enzymes in bat guano may also have important uses. They may be used to produce an alcohol fuel, and to make a substance that controls insects without harming the environment.

According to Dr. Steele, "An ounce of bat guano contains billions of bacteria, and a single tablespoon of guano may contain thousands of bacterial species, most of which we know nothing about. When a cave-dwelling bat colony is lost," he adds, "thousands of other species may also perish without our ever even knowing their actual or potential benefits."

Other scientists have been able to study vaccines and test drugs using bats. The wings of bats are so thin that they are nearly **transparent**. With a light shining behind the wing, the blood vessels and bones are clearly visible. Scientists can look at the wings under lighted microscopes without hurting the bats. In this way they can see bacteria growing or being killed by drugs while the bacteria are passing through the blood vessels in the wing.

Scientists have also studied the wing **membranes**, or thin layers of skin, to find out what effect drugs have on the blood vessels and nerves. They also hope to learn if drugs help or hinder tissue repair and regrowth of muscle.

Some bats seem to be especially good at protecting themselves against viruses and other types of infection. These bats are able to hibernate, or lower their body temperature, to survive when food is scarce. Scientists are studying them to find out if they are able to resist infection by raising or lowering their body temperature.

Medical studies of hibernating bats may help scientists interested in the effects of space travel on humans. When bats hibernate, they age more slowly.

A vampire bat makes tiny cuts with its razor-sharp teeth to feed on the blood of cattle and other animals in Central and South America.

They also resist the harmful effects of radiation much more than when they are in an active state.

Even vampire bats have been the subject of research studies. Scientists have found that the vampires' **saliva**, the thin watery liquid found in the mouth, contains a substance that dissolves blood clots. This could be helpful in treating heart attack victims.

Vampire bats usually feed on cattle and other animals commonly found in Central and South America. While the animals are asleep, the bats make tiny cuts with their razor-sharp teeth on thin-skinned areas of the animals' bodies. Vampires do not suck blood. Instead, they bite and then lap the blood as it drips from small wounds. Their saliva contains an **anticoagulant**, a substance that keeps the blood flowing so that the bats may drink their fill without waking the cattle. Many of these wounds bleed for four to six hours after the vampires have fed. Because this natural anticoagulant keeps blood from clotting, scientists believe it may be safer and more effective than the current treatment for heart attacks.

Desert Pollinators

In the deserts of the southwestern United States and Mexico, several species of agave plants and giant cacti depend on bats for pollination. At night, long-nosed bats fly from one plant to the other to feed on the nectar in the blossoms. As

A long-nosed bat feeds on the nectar in the blossoms of an agave plant.

they do so, they collect pollen on their fur and carry it from one plant to another. Many scientists believe that without bats, few agave plants or giant cacti would be pollinated. Recently, the bats that pollinate these plants and spread their seeds were declared endangered. If the bats are in danger, so are the plants that depend on them.

Without the wild agaves and giant cacti, scientists fear that the whole natural balance of the desert could be upset. Besides the long-nosed bats, moths, hummingbirds, bees, and probably many more animals and insects depend on the agave and giant cacti for food and shelter.

Tropical Pollinators

Fruit and nectar-eating bats are among the most important pollinators and seed-dispersing animals in the tropics. They spread seed by eating large amounts of fruit and expelling the solid matter, including seeds, while in flight. Without bats, plants such as bananas, plantains, peaches, breadfruit, mangoes, guavas, figs, avocados, cashews, cloves, chicle, balsa wood, and kapok would not survive in the wild. Timber from the iroko tree of West Africa, and fruit from the durian tree of Southeast Asia, are also valuable natural resources. Each is worth more than $100 million per year to the countries in which it grows. Both trees depend on bats for pollination. The African baobab tree, which is home to many kinds of wildlife, is also pollinated by bats.

In recent years, people have cut down and burned large areas of rain forests around the world. Bats play a key role in the re-seeding of areas that have been clear-cut, or stripped, of trees. In West Africa, bats carry nearly all the seeds of plants that start new growth on patches of forest that have been cleared. These "pioneer plants" are hardy trees and shrubs. They grow quickly and soon attract small mammals and birds. Then the animals bring other types of seeds which also begin to grow.

Without bats, regrowth of forest on clear-cut land might never occur. Even so, the process takes a very long time. When large areas of rain forests are cleared, entire systems of plant and animal life may be forever lost. Plants may eventually grow on the stripped area. But the great variety of plant and animal life now in the rain forest will never again be found. The relationship between plants and the animals that pollinate them and spread their seeds is complex. Scientists say it can take many thousands of years to develop. Then, if disturbed, it can take many more thousands of years to begin to recover, if recovery is possible.

If rain forests are not protected, scientists fear that their loss will contribute to the problem of global warming. This increase in the average worldwide yearly temperature could greatly change the way we all live. Only slight rises in temperature can affect crop production, water levels near coastlines, rainfall, and many other things we now take for granted.

In spite of the many ways bats are important to science and the world's environment, they are in great danger. They suffer from the loss of the natural areas where they live, and from pollution in the environment. But the greatest threat they face is the careless deeds of people.

6 Bats in Trouble

Many species of bats are endangered.

Others have already disappeared from the earth—they are now **extinct.**

Thirty years ago, the largest bat colony in the Americas was located in the southwestern United States. At that time, almost 30 million bats lived in Eagle Creek Cave. Together, they ate more than 500,000 pounds (227,000 kilograms) of insects each night. But by the 1980s, only 30,000 bats remained in the cave.

In South and Central America, thousands of roosts have been destroyed in recent years. In Europe, conditions are equally grim. Poland's bat populations have declined by 99 percent in the last forty years. In western Germany, they have dropped 90 percent in the past fifteen years.

What is happening to the bats? They are losing their roosting sites, and it takes thousands of years for bats to adapt to new ones. Most are dying because of the thoughtlessness and even purposeful acts of people.

Bats have a greater risk of becoming extinct than other animals because they roost in colonies and reproduce slowly. Most bats give birth to only one pup each year. Some do not give birth until they are five years old. During hibernation, as many as 300 adult bats can roost in one square foot of space. If only one cave is destroyed or disturbed as a roosting site, the species that roosts there may be endangered.

Loss of Roosting Sites

Mines, which could serve as sites for bat roosts, are sometimes closed off or sealed after mining operations are complete. Many cities have torn down old buildings that served as roost sites. These have sometimes been replaced by new

A colony of roosting straw-colored fruit bats. Some species of bats are endangered because many of their roosting sites have been destroyed by people.

buildings that are not suitable for bat colonies.

In both North America and Europe, forestry services often cut down dead or hollow trees. This practice has greatly reduced the numbers of tree-dwelling bats.

Vandalism

Huge colonies have been killed by people who set off cherry bombs, firecrackers, and shotguns in bat caves and mines. Many young bats die when nursery colonies are disturbed. The mothers are so frightened that they leave, abandoning their babies.

Pesticides

Chemical **pesticides** are often used to get rid of insect pests. After a time, the insects build up a resistance to a pesticide and come back in greater numbers than before. Then, the chemical builds up in the fatty tissues of the insects, even though it no longer kills them. When bats, birds, and other animals eat these insects, they eat the chemicals as well. Sometimes adult bats are not immediately affected. But young bats often die when the chemicals are passed through their mother's milk.

Bats store large amounts of fat for use during hibernation and migration. Chemicals eaten along with the insects are stored in the bats' fat. When these fat stores are used, enough chemicals often are released to kill bats or disable them so severely that they eventually die.

Eating Bats

People in parts of Asia, Africa, and some Pacific islands consider bats to be a special food. Restaurants there charge as much as $25 a plate for a flying fox—fur, bones, and all—cooked in coconut milk. Because hunters can make as much as $500 a day supplying bats to restaurants that serve them, bats are killed by the thousands to meet the demand. As a result, large flying foxes are declining rapidly.

Fear of Crop Damage

Fruit bats eat only strong-smelling fruit that is too ripe to be harvested for commercial use. Still, some people in Australia, the Middle East, and other areas believe fruit bats destroy their crops. Usually, damage blamed on bats is caused by birds or rats. And yet, thousands of bats have been killed by dynamite, flame throwers, and even napalm bombs.

In Australia, bat shoots are held in areas where bats are rearing their young. The sound of the guns frightens the mother bats away. But they return to their young even though the shooting continues. The mothers are shot one-by-one until finally none are left. The babies cannot survive without the mothers.

Many Australians do not know that these bats pollinate eucalyptus trees. Without them, koalas—prized and admired by people everywhere—will not survive. Koalas feed only on eucalyptus leaves.

Pe'a' the Rescued Flying Fox

During the summer of 1988, three American scientists were studying flying foxes in Samoa (an island in the Pacific Ocean). Shortly after they arrived, a local woman gave them a flying fox baby whose mother had been killed by hunters.

The scientists took the bat to their hotel. For several weeks they fed her baby formula and mashed bananas every two hours, night and day. They named the little bat Pe'a', which means bat in Samoan.

70

During the day, while the scientists were in the field, Pe'a' liked to roost in the hotel room on a stick placed between two tables. After a few weeks, the scientists decided to try leaving a bowl of baby formula on the table for Pe'a' to lap up instead of trying to feed her by hand every few hours. Pe'a' did well drinking from the bowl. Soon the scientists decided to leave it out for her at night as well. By morning the bowl was almost always empty.

One night Pe'a' drank all the formula and wanted more. The little bat had not yet learned to fly. Instead, she crawled down the table leg, across the floor, up the blankets, and onto the bed of the man who had been setting the milk out each night. Pe'a' then began tapping the man gently on the face with her wing. Finally, the scientist awakened and gave Pe'a' more milk.

Once Pe'a' had figured out how to get attention during the night, the little bat continued to tap the scientists' faces. Sometimes she wanted to practice flying or simply wanted attention.

Pe'a' became so tame that the scientists felt

Pe'a' the flying fox was rescued and raised by scientists in Samoa and brought back to the United States.

the little bat could not survive in the wild. They brought her back with them to the United States. Here she continues to live with one of the scientists and his family. Pe'a' has made several visits to the U.S. Congress to help publicize the need to protect the world's bats.

Hand-raised flying foxes become very attached to people who take care of them. Often, they lick

their owners' faces and even purr like cats when pet-
ted. Some Australians take care of flying foxes that
have been injured or orphaned in the wild. Once
their injuries have mended, they are set free. For
months or even years, the flying foxes will return to
visit with the people who cared for them. Sometimes they even return to show off new babies!

Bat Conservation International

A group of concerned scientists and individuals,
headed by Dr. Merlin Tuttle, has formed an organi-
zation to help protect bats worldwide. Through Bat
Conservation International (BCI), they are trying to
prevent the extinction of bats and help save species
that are declining. BCI works with governments and
conservation groups around the world. It tries to
educate people about the value and needs of bats.

One way Dr. Tuttle hopes to help the cause of
BCI is by photographing bats in their natural environment. He wants to show them as the gentle and
helpful creatures they really are.

7

A Bat Photographer

Several years ago, Dr. Merlin Tuttle was in Peru and had just recovered from a tropical fever. A Campa Indian told him about a cave deep in the jungle full of many types of bats. Dr. Tuttle was eager to take photographs of unusual bats. He lost no time assembling his cameras, lights, batteries, and other necessary equipment. With the Indian as a guide, Tuttle and his brother Arden set out on a 12-mile (19-kilometer) hike through rugged, mountainous terrain.

Nearing the mysterious cave, they came to a huge cliff nearly 200 feet (61 meters) straight down. Carrying all their gear, they climbed from ledge to ledge, clinging to vines growing out of the rocks. At the base of the cliff was a deep, clear pond. The bat cave was opposite the cliff. The only way to reach it was to swim across the pond.

Tuttle and his brother stripped to their underwear. As they plunged in the water, they noticed anaconda tracks at the water's edge. Anacondas are huge snakes that crush their prey in their coils. To their horror, the guide also mentioned that fierce fish called piranhas and electric eels lived in the depths of the pond. Struggling to keep cameras, flashlights, and batteries above the water, and feet out of the way of the dangers beneath, they swam across.

Merlin and Arden Tuttle scrambled quickly out of the water at the mouth of the cave. They were dismayed to see that oilbirds had lived just inside the cave entrance. The birds had left masses of decaying droppings. These now swarmed with huge roaches and scorpionlike insects, mites, and other mean-looking creatures.

Arden began to set up mist nets to capture any bats that might fly out of the cave. Merlin Tuttle, in his bare feet, plunged through the elbow-deep pile of bird droppings and insects. The cave floor sloped up steeply and soon narrowed to a tight crawlway so tiny that he was forced to inch along on his belly. With arms stretched in front of him, he strained his eyes in the dim glow of his flashlight to search for bats. He creeped along farther and farther to a bend in the tunnel. Hoping to reach the area where the bats roosted, he rounded the corner.

Instead of finding bats, he found a dead end with no room to turn around. Now he dripped with sweat as he fought off a growing fear of being trapped in the tight crawlway. He knew it could take hours to inch out backwards. But he told himself he could do it. Tuttle glanced over his shoulder as he backed out. Suddenly, he saw movement on the ceiling. The sight of hundreds of wriggling scorpions with stingers dangling just above his bare back made him feel sick to his stomach and nearly caused him to panic. He pressed his body tightly against the rock floor, and squeezed himself past the scorpions and out of the cave with record speed.

After all their efforts, Tuttle and his brother

found not a single bat. Fortunately, not all photographic expeditions are so disappointing or so hair-raising. But often, some danger does exist, since most bats in the wild live deep in caves or high in trees where many other types of wild animals and insects live.

During the past twelve years, Tuttle has photographed more than 300 species of bats. He has traveled to every continent, often carrying as much as 350 pounds (159 kilograms) of equipment into the back country. He has taken more than 60,000 slides of bats while studying their behavior and habits.

Capturing and Training Bats

Dr. Tuttle and his assistants capture bats in mist nets, but do not take pictures right away. Often, they will carry the bats around for hours, stroking them gently and talking to them quietly. Tuttle says that once bats are no longer afraid, they are "just as curious, winsome, and even comical as any household pet."

To get good lighting and to rid the background

Dr. Merlin Tuttle and Bert Grantges examine a bat caught in a mist net in Big Bend National Park in West Texas.

of objects that could be distracting, Tuttle sets up a portable photographic studio near his research site. Sometimes, it is outdoors and consists of a flight cage made of nets. At other times, it may be carefully placed lighting set up in a hotel room, using plastic cloth sheeting for a backdrop. A tabletop tub of water is often used to show bats skimming the water for food. Perches are built for the bats to land on.

One of Tuttle's most pleasant surprises happened when he found that bats could be trained very quickly. In fact, he discovered that it is possible to train some bats in as little as two hours from the time they are captured. With rewards of food for good behavior, they learn to come when a researcher calls. They can also be taught to respond to hand signals alone.

Once, when he helped to film a television production about bats, Tuttle trained four bats to work together. The bats each came on call and flew wherever Tuttle pointed. Frogs were placed in a small pool of water, made to look like a pond in the forest.

"Even after I had already pointed to a particular frog," said Tuttle, "the bats were trained to wait until they heard the high-speed movie camera begin, and then they caught only the individual frogs I had pointed to. Bats were trained to come from predictable directions—one always straight in, another from the left, and a third only from the right."

A Gambian epauleted bat flies toward Dr. Merlin Tuttle's camera.

Rewarding Bats

Bats do not need to be rewarded every time they perform. But after five or six performances, Tuttle has found, they pout just like some humans if not rewarded. When pouting, bats will not take even their favorite food, no matter how hungry they are. Sometimes, they will pout for half an hour before they can be coaxed into performing and accepting rewards again.

"Some people," said Tuttle, "are disappointed to learn that most bats in my pictures are tamed in captivity and often trained as well. But without such efforts the world of bats would forever remain shrouded in mystery and misunderstanding for all but a few privileged scientists."

All bats that Tuttle captures are returned to the wild. "Often," he says, "it's more difficult to say 'goodbye' to them than it is to get acquaint- ed." But he likes to think that his favorites are still alive and flying at night through the world's jun- gles. All his adventures, misadventures, and efforts are worthwhile, Tuttle believes, if his photographs help to change the harmful attitudes people have about bats.

If everyone could know that bats are gentle, in- telligent animals, we would never again have to worry about their future. We would know that bats worldwide would thrive, making our environment a better place for all plants, animals, and people.

Appendix A

Bat Houses Old and New

One of the best ways to help bats is to learn about them and tell others of their benefits to the environment. Another way is to encourage bats to live near people. They help control insects so that large amounts of chemical pesticides do not have to be used.

Europeans have been encouraging bats to live in neighborhoods for more than thirty years. They have done this by building thousands of bat houses and by placing them in yards and in national forests. But it was an American medical doctor in the early 1900s who first began experimenting with building bat houses.

Dr. Campbell's Bat Towers

Dr. Charles Campbell of San Antonio, Texas, was deeply concerned about the millions of deaths throughout the world each year caused by malaria. Dr. Campbell knew that mosquitoes carried the disease. In the farm and ranch lands around San Antonio, countless acres could not be used because swarms of mosquitoes attacked people and animals alike.

Because bats eat mosquitoes, Campbell believed they would solve the mosquito problem and stop malaria. He began to experiment with bat houses of various sizes and shapes, which he patterned after bird houses. Campbell did not succeed in attracting bats to them. After several years he decided to try building a much larger bat house—30 feet (9.1 meters) tall. Still, no bats came. Campbell was discouraged. He had spent a great deal of time, money, and effort. And yet, he had not attracted a single bat. He decided to go to the mountains of West Texas for several months to study bats and the way they live.

When Campbell returned to San Antonio, he knew much more about bats. He built another large bat tower. This time he placed it near a lake into which the city's sewage emptied. The area was a nearly perfect breeding ground for mosquitoes. In fact, there were so many of them that farmers could not work in their fields at certain times of the year. Their animals were in poor health, and nearly 90 percent of the people who lived near the lake had malaria.

Soon, bats moved into the tower. As a result, the number of mosquitoes decreased greatly, and the health of the animals improved. After four years, not a single case of malaria could be found among the people who lived near Mitchell's Lake. Campbell estimated that nearly 250,000 bats lived in that one bat tower.

In 1919, Dr. Campbell was nominated for a Nobel Prize. Soon, word of the success of the bat tower spread. By 1929, sixteen bat towers from Texas to Italy had been built.

Bat Houses in Neighborhoods and Parks

In the 1950s, people developed unfounded fears about rabies and stopped encouraging bats to live in neighborhoods. But by the 1980s, the efforts of Bat Conservation International (BCI) and news of the success Europeans were having with bat houses convinced many people in the United States and Canada to begin building bat houses again.

Bats, though, do not automatically use bat houses. They may already be roosting in a nearby attic or barn. But once bats live in the house, the same bats may return year after year. They go not only to the same house, but to the same spot within the house. Bats are most likely to move in during late summer, when young bats are old enough to look for homes on their own.

This photograph shows the large bat tower built by Dr. Charles Campbell near San Antonio, Texas.

You Can Help Bats and Bat Researchers

Scientists and observers want to know more about the likes and dislikes of bats. Many people who have bat houses are keeping detailed records. They note how close the bat houses are to water, the size of the houses, how high above ground they are placed, what directions they face, how soon they were occupied, and by how many bats. They send this information to BCI so that scientists may learn more about bats. People who help in this research are providing valuable information that may help bats and, therefore, people, worldwide.

How to Build Your Own Bat House*

    If you would like to encourage bats to live in your neighborhood, and possibly help the scientists at BCI, try putting up a bat house. With the help of an adult, you can build one in a few hours. You can also order one ready to install from BCI.

Materials Needed

One 12-foot piece of 1-inch by 8-inch (actual measurements will be slightly smaller) untreated, rough-sided cedar

One 11-inch piece of 1-inch by 10-inch untreated, rough-sided cedar (This will be the top.)

Approximately 20 six-penny galvanized nails

Tools

Skil saw with crosscut blade

Hammer

Ruler

Tape measure

Pencil

Assembly

1. Have an adult cut the 12-foot piece of cedar into 6 pieces of the following sizes:

    a) 3 pieces that are 22 inches long (These will be the two sides and the back.)

    b) 1 piece 17-1/4 inches long (This will be the front.)

    c) 2 pieces that are 13 inches long (These will be two of the three partitions.)

    d) 1 piece 11 inches long (This will be the final partition.)

2. Take two of the 22-inch pieces and measure off 17-1/4 inches on one side of each piece. Make a pencil mark at this point.

*Plans for the bat house have been adapted, with permission, from those available through Bat Conservation International. BCI also has plans for a larger house that will hold as many as 100 bats.

    If you would like to order plans or a ready-built bat house, contact BCI at P.O. Box 162603, Austin, Texas, 78716-2603.

3. Draw a diagonal line from the mark to the closest corner on the other side of the board.

4. Repeat Step 3 on the second piece.

5. Have your adult helper use a skil saw to cut along the diagonal lines. Set these pieces aside for the moment. (These will be the sides.)

6. Have your adult helper adjust the skil saw to a 33-degree angle. Take the third 22-inch board (the one you didn't mark a diagonal line on) and angle off one of the ends. This piece will be the back of the box. Repeat the same for the front piece, top piece, and for the two partitions.

7. Take the two side pieces from Step 5 and, using a ruler and pencil, mark both pieces according to the measurements shown in this figure. Mark both sides of both boards.

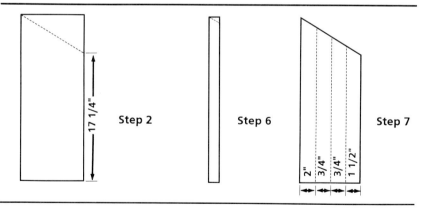

8. You're ready to start building. Take the two sides, the 22-inch back, and the 17-1/4-inch front and nail them together as illustrated, angled ends up. (Note that the side pieces fit over the ends of the front and back pieces.)

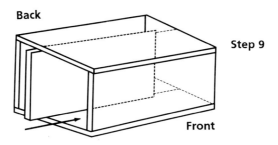

Back

Step 9

Front

---

9. Now you can insert the partitions. Lay the partially completed house on its side. Take the 13-inch internal partition and slide it into the box, centering it along the set of pencil lines closest to the back of the box. Position the partition so that it is flush with the tops of the sides.

10. Secure the partition in place with nails from the outside lines as a guide for nail placement.

11. Follow the same procedure for securing both of the shorter partitions along the other two sets of lines near the front of the box.

12. Place the 10-inch (1-inch by 10-inch) board on top so that the back edge of the board is flush with the back of the box and creates an overhang in the front and on the sides. Hold firmly and nail the top to the main frame. The completed house should look like the drawing below.

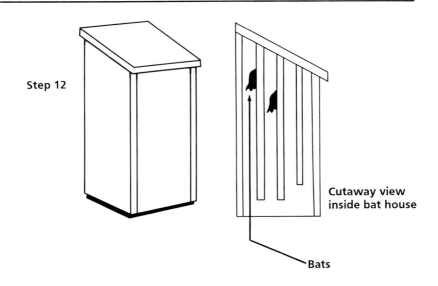

Step 12

Cutaway view inside bat house

Bats

Hanging Your Bat House

Your house can be hung in a variety of ways. One of the easiest ways is to drill two 1/4-inch holes in the back of the box. The holes should be centered and about 4 inches from the top and bottom. Drive two stout nails into the desired tree or wall, and hang the house by placing the holes over the nails. Hooks or hangers can also be used. Use your imagination!

About Bat Houses

Mother bats normally prefer the temperatures in the 80° to 100°F (27°C to 38°C) range, though some bats will roost in warmer temperatures. A nursery colony may include thirty or more bats in one house. Groups of males tend to be smaller, sometimes consisting of half a dozen or fewer bats. These often select cooler roosts.

Bat houses located near a permanent source of water, especially a marsh, lake, or river, are the most likely to attract bats. They should be hung roughly 12 to 15 feet (3.7 to 4.6 meters) above the ground, sheltered as much as possible from the wind. Don't be discouraged if conditions for your bat house are not perfect. Even natural roosts are seldom ideal.

Bats have sometimes moved in within hours. More often, though, they take as long as one or two years. If your bat house is not occupied by the end of the second year, try moving it to a warmer or cooler location. In some areas, heavy use of pesticides, a lack of hibernating sites, too great a distance to feeding or drinking sites, or too many already available summer roosting sites may cause a bat house to remain unoccupied.

Appendix B

Endangered and Threatened Bats

The following names of bats appear on the list of endangered and threatened species published by the U.S. Department of the Interior. Many other bat species are in trouble, though their names do not appear here. In the past seventeen years, nearly 300 species of plants and animals were declared extinct while awaiting government approval to be included on the list.

Bulmer's fruit bat (flying fox)
Bumblebee bat
Hawaiian hoary bat
Indiana bat
Little Mariana fruit bat
Mariana fruit bat
Mexican long-nosed bat
Ozark big-eared bat
Rodrigues fruit bat (flying fox)
Sanborn's long-nosed bat
Singapore roundleaf horseshoe bat
Virginia big-eared bat

Glossary

anticoagulant (AN-tee-koh-AG-yuh-lunt)—a substance that delays or prevents blood from clotting

bacteria (bak-TEER-ee-uh)—tiny plants that can be seen only by using a microscope. Some kinds of bacteria cause disease, while others are helpful to humans and the environment. They are found almost everywhere in the air, water, soil, and in plants and animals.

carnivorous (kahr-NIHV-uhr-uhs)—used here to mean an animal that eats the flesh of animals. Cats, dogs, wolves, and some birds and bats are carnivorous

Chiroptera (ky-RAHP-tuhr-uh)—the order of mammals that has hands which form wings; bats

creche (KREHSH)—an area within a nursery colony where baby bats are placed by their mothers

echolocation (EHK-oh-lo-KAY-shuhn)—a means of finding objects in the dark by sending high-frequency sounds and listening for their echoes

enzymes (EHN-zymz)—substances produced by living organisms (plants or animals) that cause or speed up reactions in the organisms without causing change to themselves

extinct (ek-STINKT)—no longer living anywhere on earth

fertilize (FUHRT-uh-lyz)—to join the egg (female cell) and sperm (male cell) to produce young

guano (GWAH-noh)—the waste matter of bats

hibernate—to change from a normal level of body function to a state of reduced activity, produced by the lowering of body temperature. Hibernation occurs during winter and allows some animals, including bats, to live on stored fat

mammals—warm-blooded animals that have backbones. Most are covered with fur or have hair. Females have glands that provide milk for their young

Megachiroptera (MEHG-uh-ky-RAHP-tuhr-uh)—the suborder of Chiroptera (bats) that has one family, the flying foxes. They are found in tropical and subtropical climates of Asia, Africa, and Australia (not in the Americas)

membranes (MEHM-braynz)—thin layers of skin or tissue

Microchiroptera (MY-kroh-ky-RAHP-tuhr-uh)—the suborder of Chiroptera (bats) that includes all bats except the flying foxes. All bats in the Americas are in this suborder. They live everywhere bats are found

migrate (MY-grayt)—to move from one place to another. Some bats and birds migrate to warmer climates for the winter

mist nets—nets for capturing bats that are made of very fine, hardly visible threads

nectar—a sweet liquid formed in flowers

nocturnal (nahk-TURN-ihl)—active at night

nose leaves—flaps of skin near the nose of many microbats. They help bats navigate and find food

nursery colonies—places where female bats go to bear and raise young. Bats crowd onto the walls and ceilings of caves or other protected places in such numbers that a warm environment is created for the babies

pesticides (PEHS-tuh-sydz)—substances used to kill harmful insects and other types of pests

pollen (PAHL-uhn)—a yellowish powder produced by flowers. It is made of male reproductive cells which fertilize female cells of other plants to form seeds

predators (PREHD-uh-tuhrz)—animals that hunt other animals for food

prey (PRAY)—an animal that is hunted by another animal for food

primates (PRY-maytz)—the highest order of mammals, including monkeys, apes, and humans

saliva (suh-LY-vuh)—a clear, watery liquid produced in the mouth. It keeps the mouth moist and aids in chewing and digestion

sonar (SOH-nahr)—a navigational system using sound. Echolocation used by bats, dolphins, and other animals is a natural sonar system

species (SPEE-sheez)—a group of plants or animals with common characteristics. Bluejays and robins are different species of birds

transparent (trans-PEHR-uhnt)—allowing light to pass through so that objects on the other side are easily seen

vaccines (vak-SEENZ)—germs of some diseases that are killed or weakened, then injected into humans or animals to protect them from these illnesses. Polio and smallpox vaccines are commonly given to prevent people from getting those diseases

Bibliography

Books

Fenton, Brock M., Paul Racey, and Jeremy M. Rayner, eds. *Recent Advances in the Study of Bats.* Cambridge, England: Cambridge University Press, 1987.

Hill, John E., and James D. Smith. *Bats, A Natural History.* Austin, Texas: University of Texas Press, 1984.

Hopf, Alice L. *Bats.* New York: Dodd, Mead, 1985.

Kunz, Thomas E., ed. *Ecological and Behavioral Methods for the Study of Bats.* Washington, D.C.: Smithsonian Institution Press, 1988.

Pringle, Laurence. *Vampire Bats.* New York: William Morrow, 1982.

Tuttle, Merlin D. *America's Neighborhood Bats.* Austin, Texas: University of Texas Press, 1988.

Magazines and Journals

Ackerman, Diane. "A Reporter at Large (Bats)." *The New Yorker.* (29 February 1988):37-62.

Belwood, Jacqueline J. "Sounds of Silence." *Bats* (Summer 1988):5-9.

Churchman, Deborah. "The Boy Who Became Batman." *Ranger Rick* (October 1989):18-27.

Cohn, Jeffrey P. "Applauding the Beleaguered Bat." *Americas* (November-December 1987):14-17.

Engel, Thom. "Night Flyers." *The Conservationist* (May-June 1989).

Heacox, Kim. "Fatal Attraction?" *International Wildlife* (May-June 1989):39-43.

Lenz, Mary. "Bats Aren't Bad." *Boys Life* (April 1989):11.

McCracken, Gary F., and Mary K. Gustin. "Batmom's Daily Nightmare." *Natural History* (October 1987):66-72.

Murphy, Mari. "Dr. Campbell's Malaria-Eradicating Guano-Producing Bat Roosts." *Bats* (Summer 1989):1-13.

Novacek, Michael J. "Navigators of the Night." *Natural History* (October 1988):67-70.

"Pe'a's Story." *Bats* (Fall 1988):3-4.

Rosen, Eric. "Symbiotic Life in the Desert: How a Bat and Plant Coexist." *Science Digest* (April 1980):54-57.

Steele, D. Bernie. "Bats, Bacteria and Biotechnology." *Bats* (Spring 1989):3-4.

Strohm, Bob. "Most 'Facts' about Bats are Myths." *National Wildlife* 20 (5) 1982:35-39.

Tuttle, Merlin D. "The Amazing Frog-Eating Bat." *National Geographic* (January 1982):78-91.

_____."Extending an Invitation to Bats." *Bats* (Summer 1989): 5-9.

_____. Gentle Fliers of the African Night." *National Geographic* (April 1986):544-557.

_____. "Harmless, Highly Beneficial, Bats Still Get a Bum Rap." *Smithsonian* (January 1984):74-81.

_____. "Photographing the World's Bats: Adventure, Tribulation and Rewards." *Bats* (Winter 1988):4-7.

Williams, Ted. "On Behalf of Bats." *Audubon* (September 1984): 16-19.

Interviews

O'Neill, William, Ph.D. (neuroscientist). Telephone interview with the author from the Center for Brain Research at the University of Rochester, June 1990.

Steele, D. Bernie, Ph.D. (Senior Research Associate). Telephone interview with the author from the Department of Botany and Microbiology at Auburn University, March 1990.

Tuttle, Merlin D. (founder and director of BCI). Interview with the author at Bat Conservation International, March 1989.

Index